The Sock Monster

Written by: Valeen Hall

Illustrated by: Erin Baldree

To Everyone that Made This Possible

Archway Publishing books may be ordered through booksellers or by contacting:

Archway Publishing
1663 Liberty Drive
Bloomington, IN 47403
www.archwaypublishing.com
1 (888) 242-5904

ISBN: 978-1-4808-3638-9 (sc)
ISBN: 978-1-4808-3639-6 (e)

Print information available on the last page.

Archway Publishing rev. date: 09/08/2016

Mom says there's a sock monster living in our dryer.

She doesn't know what it looks like because she's never really seen it.

She doesn't know what it
sounds like because she's
never really heard it.

But she knows it's there because every time she washes our clothes, that sock monster gobbles up some of our favorite socks.

Mom tries to fool the monster in our dryer by pinning the socks together or by washing them by themselves, but the sock monster always seems to get the best of her.

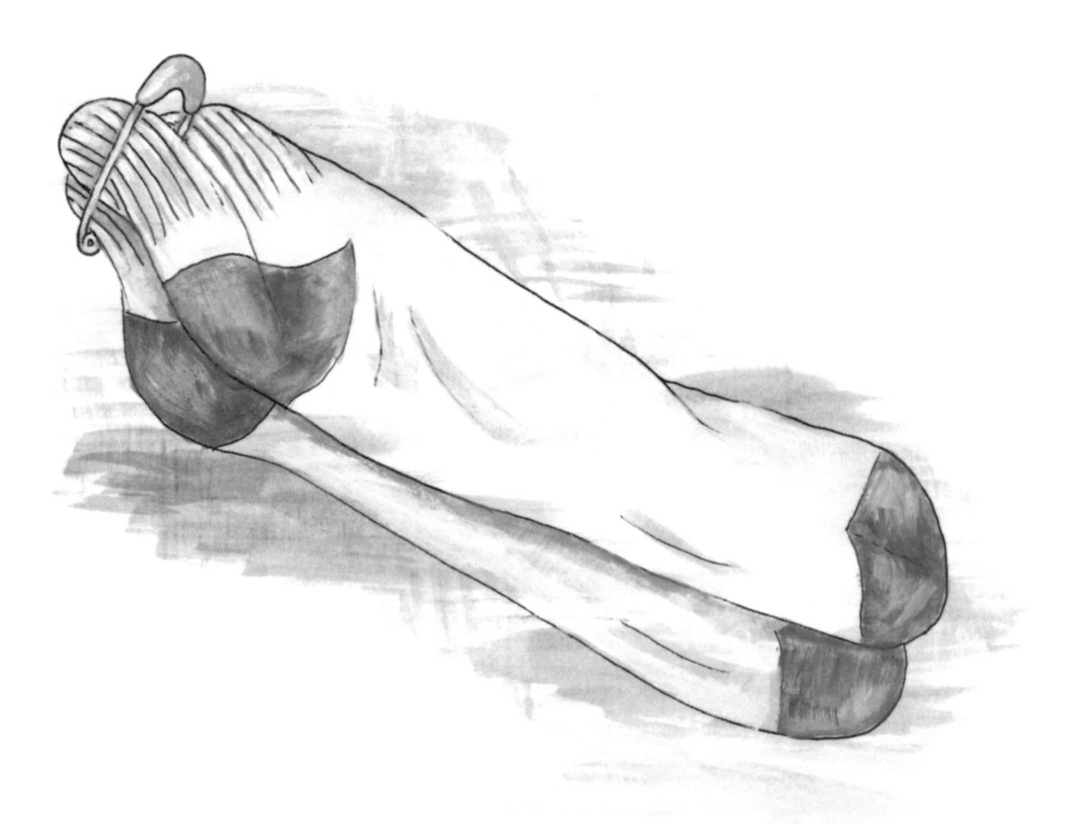

It especially likes our new socks or the socks that match our clothes.

Sometimes, when it's not very hungry, it hides our socks in strange places. . .

Sweet-O
original
whole Grains
Yum!

. . . like in our clothes. . .

. . . or even outside in the yard!

Once, my best friend brought back a sock that the sock monster had hidden at his house.

Mom says that one day she's going to get rid of that old sock monster.

KEEP OUT!
CAUTION
CAUTION
CAUTION
CAUTION
CAUTION

When we get older and move away from home, she'll have more time to catch it and send it on its way.

In the mean time we'll just have to get use to having a sock monster in our house.

Now, if only she could catch the elf who leaves all those empty milk cartons in our refrigerator.

2%

Printed in the United States
by Baker & Taylor Publisher Services